EAGLES IN THE END ZONE

By Heidi E. Y. Stemple
Illustrated by Eva Byrne

Ready-to-Read

Simon Spotlight
New York   London   Toronto   Sydney   New Delhi

To Dennis, because . . . football! —H. E. Y. S.
For my wonderful son, Dylan xxx —E. B.

SIMON SPOTLIGHT

An imprint of Simon & Schuster Children's Publishing Division

1230 Avenue of the Americas, New York, New York 10020

This Simon Spotlight edition August 2023

Text copyright © 2023 by Heidi E. Y. Stemple

Illustrations copyright © 2023 by Eva Byrne

For information about special discounts for bulk purchases, please contact
Simon & Schuster Special Sales at 1-866-506-1949 or
business@simonandschuster.com.

The Simon & Schuster Speakers Bureau can bring authors to your live event. For
more information or to book an event contact the Simon & Schuster Speakers Bureau
at 1-866-248-3049 or visit our website at www.simonspeakers.com.

Manufactured in the United States of America 0723 LAK

10 9 8 7 6 5 4 3 2 1

Library of Congress Cataloging-in-Publication Data

Names: Stemple, Heidi E. Y., author. | Byrne, Eva, illustrator.

Title: Eagles in the end zone / by Heidi E. Y. Stemple ; illustrated by Eva Byrne.

Description: Simon Spotlight edition. | New York : Simon Spotlight, 2023. |

Series: Ready-to-read: Level 1 | Audience: Ages 4 to 6. |

Summary: Birds fill the stands to watch a thrilling flag football match between the
Eagles and Turkeys—and one chicken.

Identifiers: LCCN 2022051714 (print) | LCCN 2022051715 (ebook) |

ISBN 9781665938389 (hardcover) | ISBN 9781665938372 (paperback) |

ISBN 9781665938396 (ebook)

Subjects: CYAC: Stories in rhyme. | Flag football—Fiction. | Sportsmanship—Fiction. |
Birds—Fiction. | LCGFT: Stories in rhyme. | Animal fiction. | Picture books.

Classification: LCC PZ8.3.S8228 Eag 2023 (print) | LCC PZ8.3.S8228 (ebook) |
DDC [E]—dc23

LC record available at https://lccn.loc.gov/2022051714

LC ebook record available at https://lccn.loc.gov/2022051715

Helmets.

Flags.

Pads.

Moms, chicks, dads.

The band plays loud
to rally the crowd.

Flag football! Hooray!

The big game is today!

The Eagles make a huddle.

The Turkeys make one too.

Team captains tell the players where to go and what to do.

The referee flips a coin.

The Turkeys get the ball.

Cheerleaders make a pyramid three flamingos tall.

TWEET!

Hike the ball.

Throw the ball.

Run,

run,

run!

The fans order hot dogs.
Everyone is having fun.

Touchdown for the home team.

Touchdown for the other.

The score is adding up,
until . . .

Chicken spots his grandmother.

A wing is raised to wave hello.

Oh no,

oh no . . .

Oh no, no,

Hot dogs drop.

Instruments rumble.

Every player runs around hoping to catch the fumble.

TWEET!

Referee yells, "Stop!
That ball is not in play."
But no one on the field
hears what she has to say.

The football is recovered . . .

by who?

By . . .

Chicken?

Wrong way, Chicken!
That is the wrong side!

But Grandma in the stands
is filled with game-day pride!

SCORE?

No score!

The big game ends in a tie,
but no one seems to care.

Together they lift Chicken high up in the air.

Both teams award Chicken the Good Sportsmanship prize.

And he is the MVP*

in his grandmother's eyes.

*most valuable player